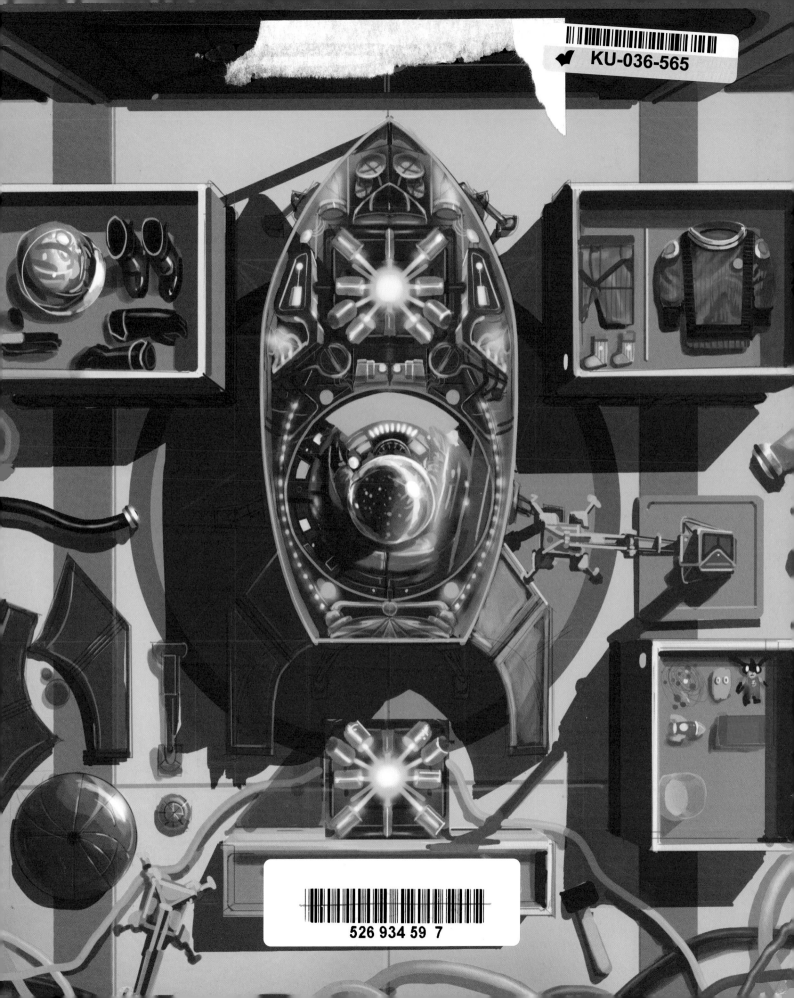

TINY LITTLE ROCKET is a DAVID FICKLING BOOK

First published in Great Britain in 2018 by David Fickling Books,
31 Beaumont Street, Oxford, OX1 2NP

978 1 910200 90 2

www.davidficklingbooks.com

Text © David Fickling, 2018

Illustrations © Richard Collingridge, 2018

1 3 5 7 9 10 8 6 4 2

The right of David Fickling and Richard Collingridge to be identified
as the author and illustrator of this work has been asserted in
accordance with the Copyright, Designs and Patents Act 1988.
All rights reserved.

WARNING: This book will make you want to BLAST OFF into
outer space!

Papers used by David Fickling Books are from well-managed forests
and other responsible sources.

DAVID FICKLING BOOKS Reg. No. 8340307

A CIP catalogue record for this book is available from the British Library.

Design *et al* design consultants. Printed and bound in China by Toppan Leefung

# Tiny Little Rocket

## David Fickling & Richard Collingridge

David Fickling Books

There's a tiny little rocket
that will take you to the stars.

It only flies there once a year,
but zips you out past Mars.

Its fins are solid silver
with a door made out of gold.

There's a cosy pilot seat inside
for a person, young or old.

It whizzes out to deepest space
while you hold on by the handle.

And there you'll find the golden sun,
our ever burning candle.

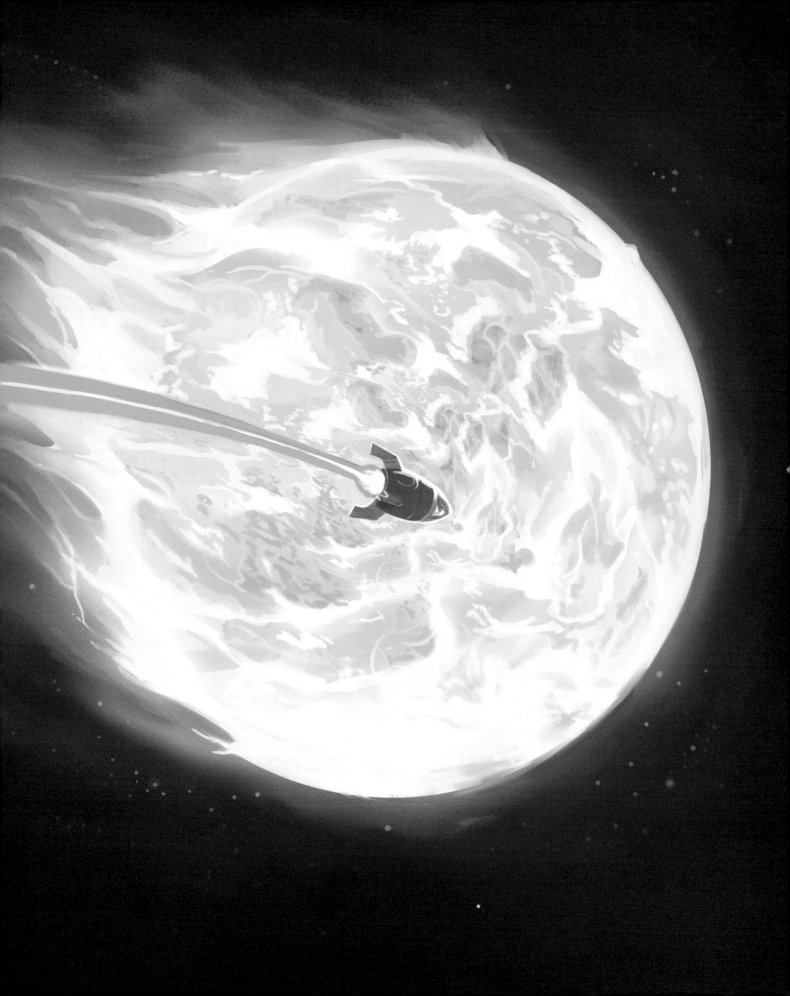

You hang there for a moment
while the rocket hums and clicks.

The sunlight gleams on silver wings;
behind you something ticks.

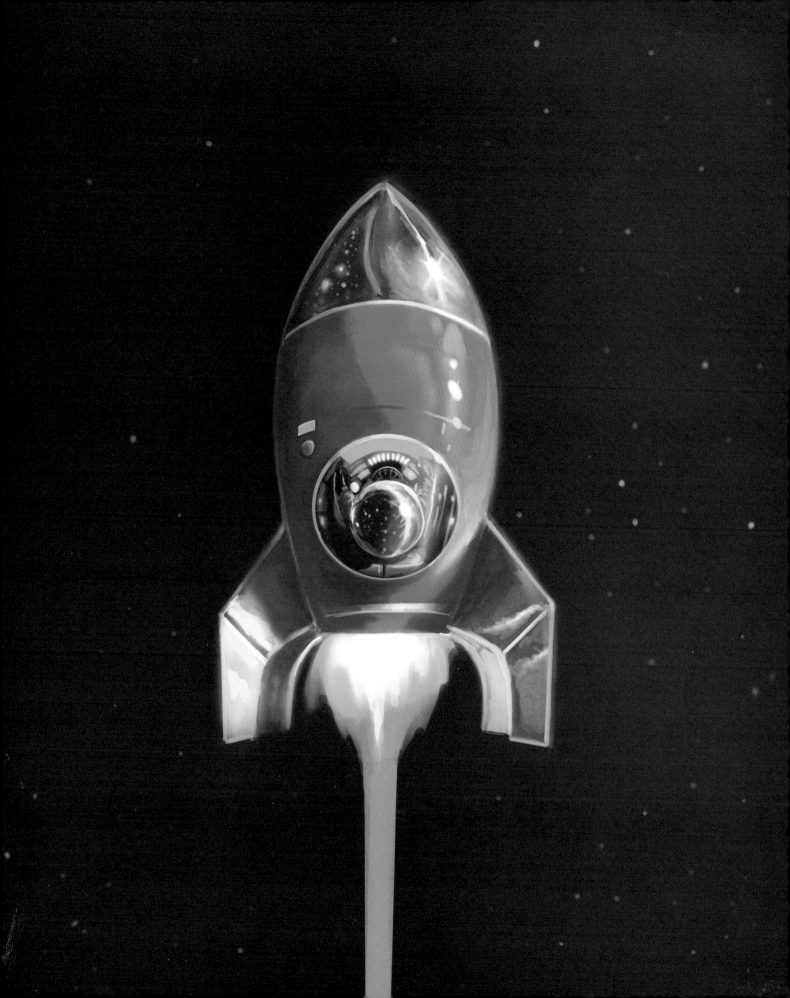

You see a purple lever
that blares out
**PULL ME NOW!**

The booster rockets all go
**WHOOSH!**

You quietly whisper,
**WOW!**

The little rocket zooms again,

A **HUGE** rock fills the screen.
A **METEOR!**
It's going to **HIT!**

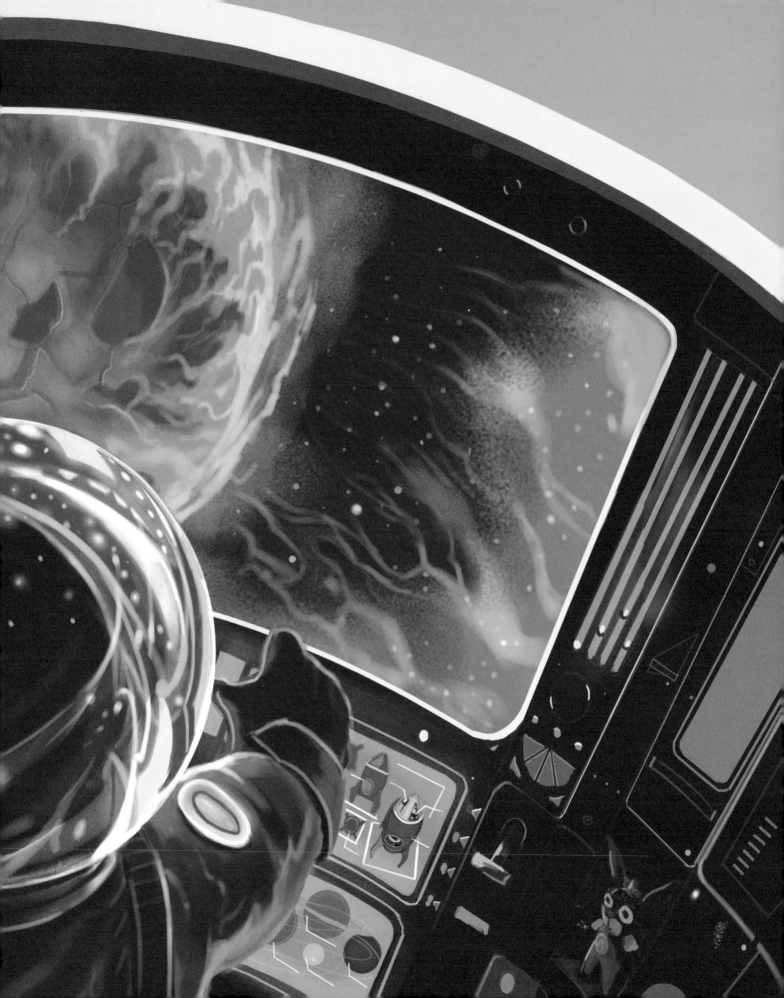

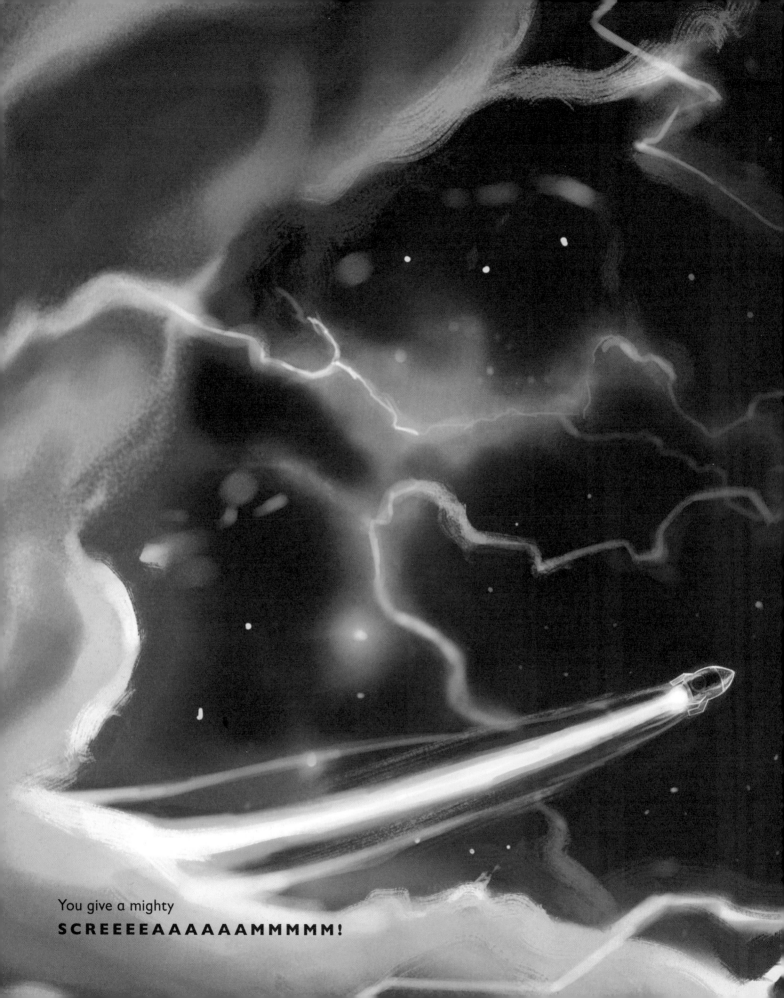

You give a mighty
**SCREEEEAAAAAAMMMMM!**

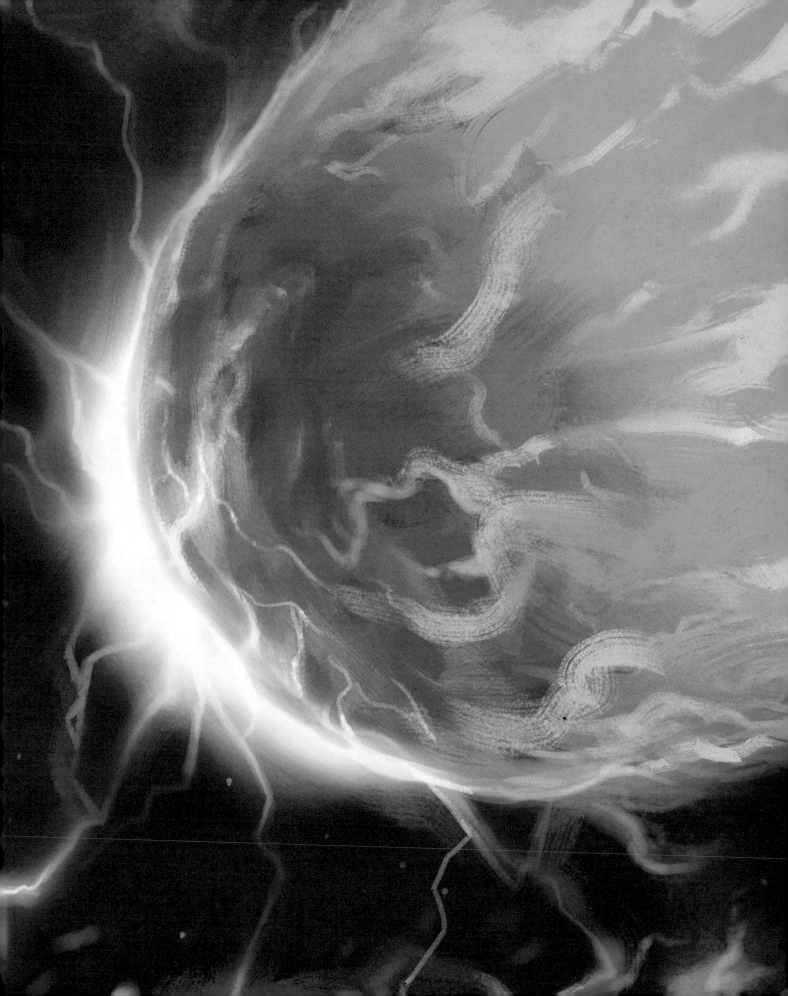

It bops the rocket in the face
and knocks you into outer space!

Round and round the stars do roll,

**QUICK!**

You'd better take control . . .

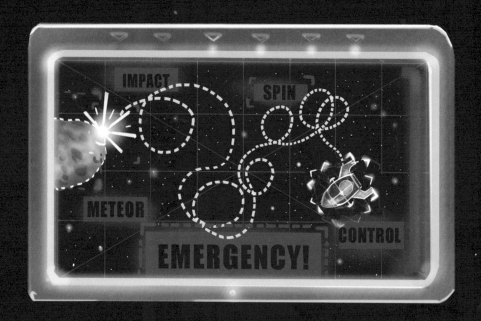

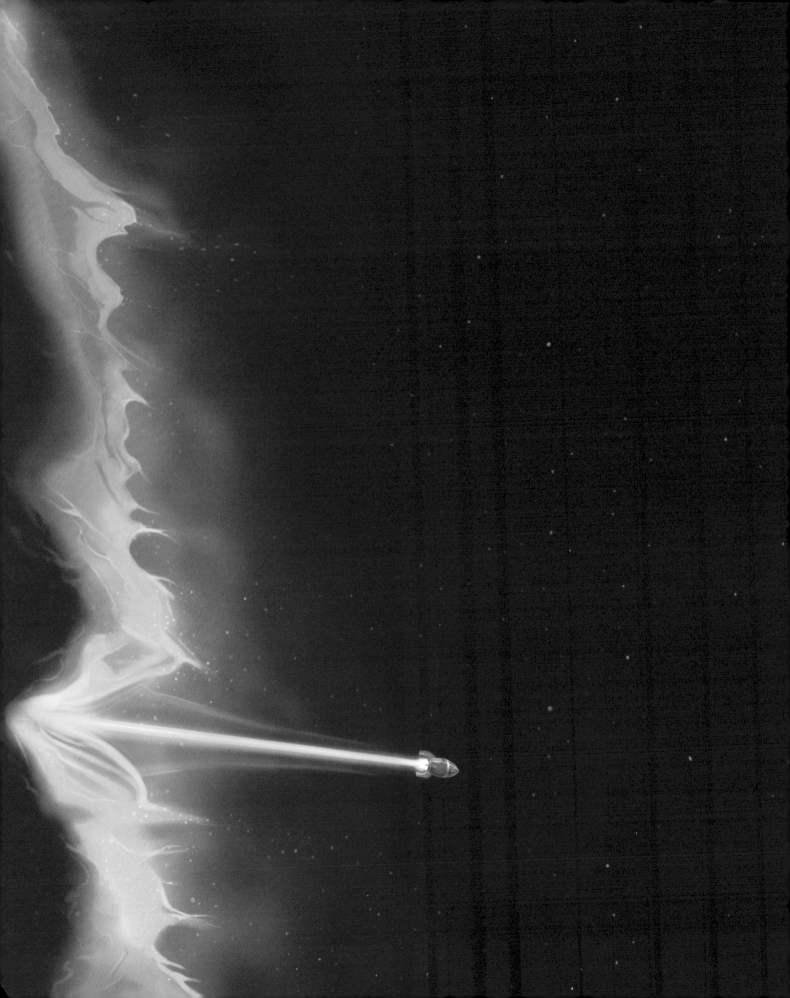

You turn the wheel,
you steer the ship,
your eyes go wide to see.

And like a gorgeous fish of steel
in space you're swimming free!

You dive back through our system,
each planet one by one.

The tiny rocket **ZOOMS** you home
to the third one from the sun.

There's a button on the rocket
that winks just by your head,

and you have to press that
button when it turns from . . .

**GREEN** to **RED!**

You press the button with
your hand and . . .

. . . a banner is unfurled.
It stretches from the moon to Mars,
saying . . .